Murphy's Law

and other reasons why things go wrong!

Arthur Bloch

PRICE/STERN/SLOAN
Publishers, Inc., Los Angeles
1979

NINTH PRINTING — AUGUST, 1979

ACKNOWLEDGEMENTS AND PERMISSIONS

Grateful acknowledgement is made to the following for permission to reprint their material:

Laws of Computer Programming: "Datamation," 1968, Technical Publishing Co., Greenwich, Connecticut.

Sparks's Ten Rules for the Project Manager; Laws of Procrastination; Gordon's First Law; Maier's Law; Edington's Theory; Parkinson's Law for Medical Research; Peter's Hidden Postulate according to Godin; Godin's Law; Freeman's Rule; Old and Kahn's Law; First Law of Socio-Genetics; Hersh's Law: "Journal of Irreproducible Results," Box 234, Chicago Heights, Illinois.

Parkinson's First, Second, Third, Fourth and Fifth Laws; Parkinson's Law of Delay; Parkinson's Axioms: C. Northcote Parkinson's *Parkinson's Law, Mrs. Parkinson's Law, The Law and the Profits, The Law of Delay* and *In-Laws and Outlaws,* Houghton Mifflin Company, Boston, Massachusetts.

The Peter Principle and its Corollaries; Peter's Inversion; Peter's Placebo; Peter's Prognosis; Peter's Law of Evolution*; Peter's Observation*; Peter's Law of Substitution*; Peter's Rule for Creative Incompetence*; Peter's Theorem*: Dr. Laurence J. Peter and Raymond Hull's *The Peter Principle,* Wm. Morrow and Co., New York, 1969.
(*so named by the editors)

Very special thanks also to Conrad Schneiker for his invaluable assistance and support.

ISBN: 0-8431-0428-7

CONTENTS

PREFACE

Who was Murphy? What curious conspiracy of circumstances inspired him to formulate his now-famous precept? Why didn't he pick up his laundry? These are just a few of the many questions that I had no intention of answering in this book. Our finest scholars, experts in the fields of linguistics and folk history, have tried and failed to determine the origin of Murphy's Law. Who was I to argue with such a record?

Resigned as I was to go to print without resolving these burning questions, I was most surprised to receive the following letter from a certain Mr. George Nichols of Southern California:

Dear Arthur Bloch:

Understand you are going to publish a book, Murphy's Law — And Other Reasons Why Things Go Wrong. *Are you interested in including the true story of the naming of Murphy's Law?*

And, when I responded in the affirmative:

The event occurred in 1949 at Edwards Air Force Base, Muroc, California, during Air Force Project MX981. This was Col. J. P. Stapp's experimental crash research testing on the track at North Base. The work was being accomplished by Northrop Aircraft, under contract from the Aero Medical Lab at Wright Field. I was Northrop's project manager.

*The Law's namesake was Capt. Ed Murphy, a develop-
ment engineer from Wright Field Aircraft Lab. Frustra-
tion with a strap transducer which was malfunctioning
due to an error in wiring the strain gage bridges caused
him to remark — "If there is any way to do it wrong,
he will" — referring to the technician who had wired the
bridges at the Lab. I assigned Murphy's Law to the statement and the associated variations.*

*. . . A couple of weeks after the "naming," Col. Stapp
indicated, at a press conference, that our fine safety
record during several years of simulated crash force
testing was the result of a firm belief in Murphy's Law,
and our consistent effort to deny the inevitable. The
widespread reference to the Law in manufacturers' ads
within only a few months was fantastic — and Murphy's
Law was off and running wild.*

> *Sincerely,*
> *George E. Nichols*
> **Reliability & Quality Assurance Mgr.**
> **Viking Project**
> **Jet Propulsion Lab — NASA**

Thus, thanks to Mr. Nichols's kindly missive, the plot thins;
for here we have the answers to the aforementioned burning
questions in more detail than we would have thought
necessary. There only remains to find out why Ed Murphy
didn't pick up his laundry.

> Arthur Bloch
> Berkeley, September, 1977

INTRODUCTION

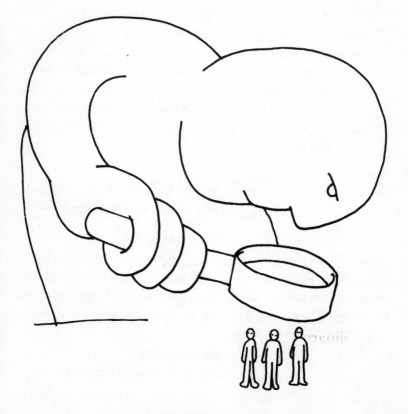

Have you ever received a phone call the minute you sat down on the toilet? Has the bus you wanted ever appeared the instant you lit up a cigarette? Has it ever started raining on the day you washed your car, or stopped raining just after you bought an umbrella? Perhaps you realized at the time that something was afoot, that some universal principle was just out of your grasp, itching to be called by name. Or perhaps, having heard of Murphy's Law, the Peter Principle or the Law of Selective Gravity, you have wanted to invoke one of these, only to find that you have forgotten its exact wording.

Here, then, is the first compilation in book form of the wit and wisdom of our most delightfully demented technologists, bureaucrats, humanists, and anti-social observers, prepared and presented with the purpose of providing us all with a little Karmic Relief. The listing has been made as definitive as possible. In researching these inter-disciplinary tenets, we found numerous redundancies (which verify the validity of the observations), frequent conflicting claims to authorship, and scores of anonymous donations. We are forced to acknowledge the contribution of the inimitable Zymurgy, who said, "Once you open a can of worms, the only way to recan them is to use a larger can." By applying this Murphic morsel to the present volume, we come to realize that this project, once undertaken, must surely grow in size and scope as further principles, new and old, are revealed by our beacon of truth.

Throughout history pundits and poseurs have regaled us with the laws of the universe, the subtle yet immutable substructure which is the basis of cosmic order. From people of religion we have received the Moral Laws; from mystics, the Laws of Karma; from rationalists, the Laws of Logical Form; and from artists, the Laws of Aesthetics. Now it is the technologists' turn to bend our collective ear.

The official party line of technology, of science itself, is despair. If you doubt this, witness the laws of thermodynamics as they are restated in Ginsberg's Theorem. The universe is simmering down, like a giant stew left to cook for four billion years. Sooner or later we won't be able to tell the carrots from the onions.

"But what of the short run, the proverbial closed system?" you may well ask, as you sit gazing out of your penthouse window, sipping your vodka martini and watching the hustling throngs of God's little creatures going about their business. Alas, we've only to look at this business, as exemplified in the good bureaucracy, through the eyes of Peter, Parkinson, et al. We will realize that it is only a matter of time before the microcosmic specks we call big business and government, like their universal counterpart, lose their ability to succeed in spite of themselves.

"We are on the wrong side of the tapestry." So said Father Brown, G. K. Chesterton's famous clerical sleuth. And indeed we are. A few loose ends, an occasional thread, are all we ever see of the great celestial masterwork of the most expensive carpet weaver of them all. A small number of courageous individuals have dared to explore the far side of the tapestry, have braved the wrath of the Keeper of the Rug in their search for truth. It is to these individuals that this volume is dedicated.

MURPHOLOGY

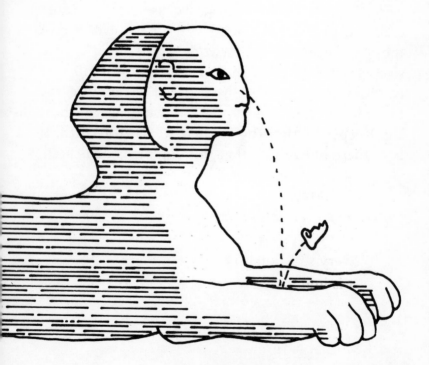

MURPHY'S LAW:

   If anything can go wrong, it will.

   Corollaries:

   1. Nothing is as easy as it looks.

   2. Everything takes longer than you think.

   3. If there is a possibility of several things going wrong, the one that will cause the most damage will be the one to go wrong.

   4. If you perceive that there are four possible ways in which a procedure can go wrong, and circumvent these, then a fifth way will promptly develop.

   5. Left to themselves, things tend to go from bad to worse.

   6. Whenever you set out to do something, something else must be done first.

   7. Every solution breeds new problems.

   8. It is impossible to make anything foolproof because fools are so ingenious.

   9. Nature always sides with the hidden flaw.

   10. Mother nature is a bitch.

THE MURPHY PHILOSOPHY:

Smile . . . tomorrow will be worse.

MURPHY'S CONSTANT:

Matter will be damaged in direct proportion
to its value.

QUANTIZATION REVISION OF MURPHY'S LAW:

Everything goes wrong all at once.

HILL'S COMMENTARIES ON MURPHY'S LAW:

1. If we lose much by having things go wrong,
   take all possible care.
2. If we have nothing to lose by change,
   relax.
3. If we have everything to gain by change,
   relax.
4. If it doesn't matter, it does not matter.

O'TOOLE'S COMMENTARY ON MURPHY'S LAW:

Murphy was an optimist.

**ZYMURGY'S SEVENTH EXCEPTION TO
MURPHY'S LAW:**

When it rains, it pours.

BOLING'S POSTULATE:

If you're feeling good, don't worry. You'll get
over it.

WHITE'S STATEMENT:

Don't lose heart . . .

Owen's Commentary on White's Statement:

. . . they might want to cut it out . . .

Byrd's Addition to Owen's Commentary on White's Statement:

. . . and they want to avoid a lengthy search.

ILES'S LAW:

There is always an easier way to do it.

Corollaries:

1. When looking directly at the easier way, especially for long periods, you will not see it.

2. Neither will Iles.

CHISHOLM'S SECOND LAW:

When things are going well, something will go wrong.

Corollaries:

1. When things just can't get any worse, they will.

2. Anytime things appear to be going better, you have overlooked something.

CHISHOLM'S THIRD LAW:

Proposals, as understood by the proposer, will be judged otherwise by others.

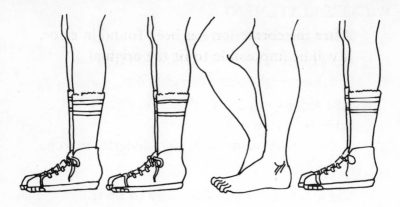

Corollaries:

1. If you explain so clearly that nobody can misunderstand, somebody will.

2. If you do something which you are sure will meet with everybody's approval, somebody won't like it.

3. Procedures devised to implement the purpose won't quite work.

SCOTT'S FIRST LAW:

No matter what goes wrong, it will probably look right.

SCOTT'S SECOND LAW:

When an error has been detected and corrected, it will be found to have been correct in the first place.

Corollary:

After the correction has been found in error, it will be impossible to fit the original quantity back into the equation.

FINAGLE'S FIRST LAW:

If an experiment works, something has gone wrong.

FINAGLE'S SECOND LAW:

No matter what the anticipated result, there will always be someone eager to (a) misinterpret it, (b) fake it, or (c) believe it happened to his own pet theory.

FINAGLE'S THIRD LAW:

In any collection of data, the figure most obviously correct, beyond all need of checking, is the mistake.

Corollaries:

1. No one whom you ask for help will see it.
2. Everyone who stops by with unsought advice will see it immediately.

FINAGLE'S FOURTH LAW:

Once a job is fouled up, anything done to improve it only makes it worse.

FINAGLE'S RULES:

1. To study a subject best, understand it thoroughly before you start.

2. Always keep a record of data — it indicates you've been working.

3. Always draw your curves, then plot your reading.

4. In case of doubt, make it sound convincing.

5. Experiments should be reproducible — they should all fail in the same way.

6. Do not believe in miracles — rely on them.

WINGO'S AXIOM:

All Finagle Laws may be bypassed by learning the simple art of doing without thinking.

GUMPERSON'S LAW:

The probability of anything happening is in inverse ratio to its desirability.

ISSAWI'S LAWS OF PROGRESS:

The Course of Progress:
Most things get steadily worse.

The Path of Progress:
A shortcut is the longest distance between two points.

The Dialectics of Progress:

Direct action produces direct reaction.

The Pace of Progress:

Society is a mule, not a car . . . If pressed too hard, it will kick and throw off its rider.

SODD'S FIRST LAW:

When a person attempts a task, he or she will be thwarted in that task by the unconscious intervention of some other presence (animate or inanimate). Nevertheless, some tasks are completed, since the intervening presence is itself attempting a task and is, of course, subject to interference.

SODD'S SECOND LAW:

Sooner or later, the worst possible set of circumstances is bound to occur.

Corollary:

Any system must be designed to withstand the worst possible set of circumstances.

SIMON'S LAW:

Everything put together falls apart sooner or later.

RUDIN'S LAW:

In crises that force people to choose among alternative courses of action, most people will choose the worst one possible.

GINSBERG'S THEOREM:

1. You can't win.
2. You can't break even.
3. You can't even quit the game.

FREEMAN'S COMMENTARY ON GINSBERG'S THEOREM:

Every major philosophy that attempts to make life seem meaningful is based on the negation of one part of Ginsberg's Theorem. To wit:

1. Capitalism is based on the assumption that you can win.
2. Socialism is based on the assumption that you can break even.
3. Mysticism is based on the assumption that you can quit the game.

EHRMAN'S COMMENTARY:

1. Things will get worse before they get better.
2. Who said things would get better?

EVERITT'S SECOND LAW OF THERMODYNAMICS:

Confusion is always increasing in society. Only if someone or something works extremely hard can this confusion be reduced to order in a limited region. Nevertheless, this effort will still result in an increase in the total confusion of society at large.

MURPHY'S LAW OF THERMODYNAMICS:

Things get worse under pressure.

COMMONER'S SECOND LAW OF ECOLOGY:

Nothing ever goes away.

PUDDER'S LAW:

Anything that begins well, ends badly.
Anything that begins badly, ends worse.

STOCKMAYER'S THEOREM:

If it looks easy, it's tough.
If it looks tough, it's damn well impossible.

HOWE'S LAW:

Everyone has a scheme that will not work.

WYNNE'S LAW:

Negative slack tends to increase.

ZYMURGY'S FIRST LAW OF EVOLVING SYSTEMS DYNAMICS:

Once you open a can of worms, the only way to recan them is to use a larger can.

STURGEON'S LAW:

90% of everything is crud.

THE UNSPEAKABLE LAW:

As soon as you mention something . . .
  . . . if it's good, it goes away.
  . . . if it's bad, it happens.

NON-RECIPROCAL LAWS OF EXPECTATIONS:

Negative expectations yield negative results.

Positive expectations yield negative results.

APPLIED
MURPHOLOGY

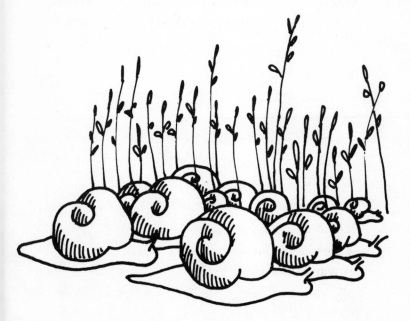

BOOKER'S LAW:

> An ounce of application is worth a ton of abstraction.

KLIPSTEIN'S LAWS:

Applied to General Engineering:

1. A patent application will be preceded by one week by a similar application made by an independent worker.

2. Firmness of delivery dates is inversely proportional to the tightness of the schedule.

3. Dimensions will always be expressed in the least usable term. Velocity, for example, will be expressed in furlongs per fortnight.

4. Any wire cut to length will be too short.

Applied to Prototyping and Production:

1. Tolerances will accumulate unidirectionally toward maximum difficulty to assemble.

2. If a project requires 'n' components, there will be 'n-l' units in stock.

3. A motor will rotate in the wrong direction.

4. A fail-safe circuit will destroy others.

5. A transistor protected by a fast-acting fuse will protect the fuse by blowing first.

6. A failure will not appear till a unit has passed final inspection.

7. A purchased component or instrument will meet its specs long enough, and only long enough, to pass incoming inspection.

8. After the last of 16 mounting screws has been removed from an access cover, it

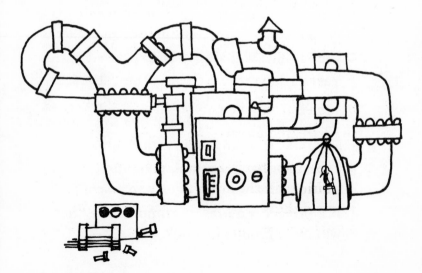

will be discovered that the wrong access cover has been removed.

9. After an access cover has been secured by 16 hold-down screws, it will be discovered that the gasket has been omitted.

10. After an instrument has been assembled, extra components will be found on the bench.

THE RECOMMENDED PRACTICES COMMITTEE OF THE INTERNATIONAL SOCIETY OF PHILOSOPHICAL ENGINEERS' UNIVERSAL LAWS FOR NAIVE ENGINEERS:

1. In any calculation, any error which can creep in will do so.

2. Any error in any calculation will be in the direction of most harm.

3. In any formula, constants (especially those obtained from engineering handbooks) are to be treated as variables.

4. The best approximation of service conditions in the laboratory will not begin to meet those conditions encountered in actual service.

5. The most vital dimension on any plan or drawing stands the greatest chance of being omitted.

6. If only one bid can be secured on any project, the price will be unreasonable.

7. If a test installation functions perfectly, all subsequent production units will malfunction.

8. All delivery promises must be multiplied by a factor of 2.0.

9. Major changes in construction will always be requested after fabrication is nearly completed.

10. Parts that positively cannot be assembled in improper order will be.

11. Interchangeable parts won't.

12. Manufacturer's specifications of performance should be multiplied by a factor of 0.5.

13. Salespeople's claims for performance should be multiplied by a factor of 0.25.

14. Installation and Operating Instructions shipped with the device will be promptly discarded by the Receiving Department.

15. Any device requiring service or adjustment will be least accessible.

16. Service Conditions as given on specifications will be exceeded.

17. If more than one person is responsible for a miscalculation, no one will be at fault.

18. Identical units which test in an identical fashion will not behave in an identical fashion in the field.

19. If, in engineering practice, a safety factor is set through service experience at an ultimate value, an ingenious idiot will promptly calculate a method to exceed said safety factor.

20. Warranty and guarantee clauses are voided by payment of the invoice.

ATWOOD'S FOURTEENTH COROLLARY:

No books are lost by lending except those you particularly wanted to keep.

JOHNSON'S THIRD LAW:

If you miss one issue of any magazine, it will be the issue which contained the article, story or installment you were most anxious to read.

Corollary:

All of your friends either missed it, lost it or threw it out.

HARPER'S MAGAZINE'S LAW:

You never find an article until you replace it.

RICHARD'S COMPLEMENTARY RULES OF OWNERSHIP:

1. If you keep anything long enough you can throw it away.
2. If you throw anything away, you will need it as soon as it is no longer accessible.

GLATUM'S LAW OF MATERIALISTIC ACQUISITIVENESS:

The perceived usefulness of an article is inversely proportional to its actual usefulness once bought and paid for.

LEWIS'S LAW:

No matter how long or how hard you shop for an item, after you've bought it it will be on sale somewhere cheaper.

PERLSWEIG'S LAW:

People who can least afford to pay rent, pay rent. People who can most afford to pay rent, build up equity.

LAWS OF GARDENING:

1. Other people's tools work only in other people's gardens.
2. Fancy gizmos don't work.
3. If nobody uses it, there's a reason.
4. You get the most of what you need the least.

McCLAUGHRY'S LAW OF ZONING:

Where zoning is not needed, it will work perfectly.

Where it is desperately needed, it always breaks down.

THE AIRPLANE LAW:

When the plane you are on is late, the plane you want to transfer to is on time.

FIRST LAW OF BICYCLING:

No matter which way you ride, it's uphill and against the wind.

FIRST LAW OF BRIDGE:

It's always the partner's fault.

RULE OF FELINE FRUSTRATION:

When your cat has fallen asleep on your lap and looks utterly content and adorable you will suddenly have to go to the bathroom.

KITMAN'S LAW:

Pure drivel tends to drive off the TV screen ordinary drivel.

JOHNSON AND LAIRD'S LAW:

Toothache tends to start on Saturday night.

ETORRE'S OBSERVATION:

The other line moves faster.

BOOB'S LAW:

You always find something the last place you look.

DESIGNSMANSHIP

OSBORN'S LAW:

Variables won't; constants aren't.

KLIPSTEIN'S LAW OF SPECIFICATION:

In specifications, Murphy's Law supersedes Ohm's.

FIRST LAW OF REVISION:

Information necessitating a change of design will be conveyed to the designer after — and only after — the plans are complete. (Often called the "Now they tell us!" Law.)

Corollary:

In simple cases, presenting one obvious right way versus one obvious wrong way, it is often wiser to choose the wrong way, so as to expedite subsequent revision.

SECOND LAW OF REVISION:

The more innocuous the modification appears to be, the further its influence will extend and the more plans will have to be redrawn.

THIRD LAW OF REVISION:

If, when completion of a design is imminent,

field dimensions are finally supplied as they actually are — instead of as they were meant to be — it is always simpler to start all over.

Corollary:

It is usually impractical to worry beforehand about interferences — if you have none, someone will make one for you.

LAW OF THE LOST INCH:

In designing any type of construction, no overall dimension can be totalled correctly after 4:40 p.m. on Friday.

Corollaries:

1. Under the same conditions, if any minor dimensions are given to sixteenths of an inch, they cannot be totalled at all.

2. The correct total will become self-evident at 9:01 a.m. on Monday.

LAWS OF APPLIED CONFUSION:

1. The one piece that the plant forgot to ship is the one that supports 75% of the balance of the shipment.

Corollary:

Not only did the plant forget to ship it, 50% of the time they haven't even made it.

2. Truck deliveries that normally take one day

will take five when you are waiting for the truck.

3. After adding two weeks to the schedule for unexpected delays, add two more for the unexpected, unexpected delays.

4. In any structure, pick out the one piece that should not be mismarked and expect the plant to cross you up.

Corollaries:

1. In any group of pieces with the same erection mark on it, one should not have that mark **on it**.

2. **It will not be discovered until you try to put it where the mark says it's supposed to go.**

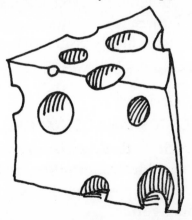

3. **Never argue with the fabricating plant about an error. The inspection prints are all checked off, even to the holes that aren't there.**

WYSZKOWSKI'S THEOREM:

Regardless of the units used by either the supplier or the customer, the manufacturer shall use his own arbitrary units convertible to those of either the supplier or the customer only by means of weird and unnatural conversion factors.

THE SNAFU EQUATIONS:

1. Given any problem containing 'n' equations, there will always be 'n+l' unknowns.
2. An object or bit of information most needed will be the least available.
3. Once you have exhausted all possibilities and fail, there will be one solution, simple and obvious, highly visible to everyone else.
4. Badness comes in waves.

SKINNER'S CONSTANT
(FLANNAGAN'S FINAGLING FACTOR):

That quantity which, when multiplied by, divided by, added to, or subtracted from the answer you get, gives you the answer you should have gotten.

MIKSCH'S LAW:

If a string has one end, then it has another end.

LAWS OF COMPUTER PROGRAMMING:

1. Any given program, when running, is obsolete.

2. Any given program costs more and takes longer.

3. If a program is useful, it will have to be changed.

4. If a program is useless, it will have to be documented.

5. Any given program will expand to fill all available memory.

6. The value of a program is proportional to the weight of its output.

7. Program complexity grows until it exceeds the capability of the programmer who must maintain it.

TROUTMAN'S PROGRAMMING POSTULATES:

1. If a test installation functions perfectly, all subsequent systems will malfunction.

2. Not until a program has been in production for at least six months will the most harmful error be discovered.

3. Job control cards that positively cannot be arranged in improper order will be.

4. Interchangeable tapes won't.

5. If the input editor has been designed to reject all bad input, an ingenious idiot will discover

a method to get bad data past it.

6. Profanity is the one language all programmers know best.

GILB'S LAWS OF UNRELIABILITY:

1. Computers are unreliable, but humans are even more unreliable.

2. Any system which depends on human reliability is unreliable.

3. Undetectable errors are infinite in variety, in contrast to detectable errors, which by definition are limited.

4. Investment in reliability will increase until it exceeds the probable cost of errors, or until someone insists on getting some useful work done.

BROOK'S LAW:

Adding manpower to a late software project makes it later.

LAWS OF COMPUTERDOM ACCORDING TO GOLUB:

1. Fuzzy project objectives are used to avoid the embarrassment of estimating the corresponding costs.

2. A carelessly planned project takes three

times longer to complete than expected;
a carefully planned project takes only twice
as long.

3. The effort required to correct course
   increases geometrically with time.

4. Project teams detest weekly progress reporting
   because it so vividly manifests their lack
   of progress.

LUBARSKY'S LAW OF CYBERNETIC ENTOMOLOGY:

There's always one more bug.

SHAW'S PRINCIPLE:

Build a system that even a fool can use, and
only a fool will want to use it.

MACHINESMANSHIP

IBM POLLYANNA PRINCIPLE:

Machines should work; people should think.

LAW OF THE PERVERSITY OF NATURE:

You cannot successfully determine beforehand which side of the bread to butter.

LAW OF SELECTIVE GRAVITY:

An object will fall so as to do the most damage.

Jenning's Corollary:

The chance of the bread falling with the buttered side down is directly proportional to the cost of the carpet.

Klipstein's Corollary:

The most delicate component will be the one to drop.

SPRINKLE'S LAW:

Things always fall at right angles.

ANTHONY'S LAW OF THE WORKSHOP:

Any tool, when dropped, will roll into the least accessible corner of the workshop.

Corollary:

On the way to the corner, any dropped tool will first always strike your toes.

THE SPARE PARTS PRINCIPLE:

The accessibility, during recovery of small parts which fall from the work bench, varies directly with the size of the part — and inversely with its importance to the completion of work underway.

PAUL'S LAW:

You can't fall off the floor.

JOHNSON'S FIRST LAW:

When any mechanical contrivance fails, it will do so at the most inconvenient possible time.

LAW OF ANNOYANCE:

When working on a project, if you put away a tool that you're certain you're finished with, you will need it instantly.

WATSON'S LAW:

The reliability of machinery is inversely proportional to the number and significance of any persons watching it.

WYSZKOWSKI'S SECOND LAW:

Anything can be made to work if you fiddle with it long enough.

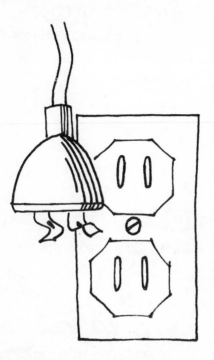

SATTINGER'S LAW:

It works better if you plug it in.

LOWERY'S LAW:

If it jams — force it. If it breaks, it needed replacing anyway.

SCHMIDT'S LAW:

If you mess with a thing long enough,
it'll break.

FUDD'S FIRST LAW OF OPPOSITION:

Push something hard enough and it will
fall over.

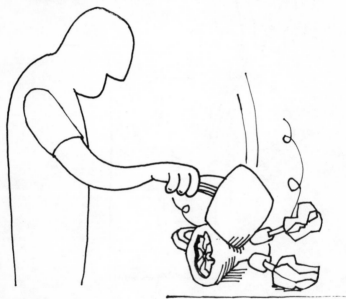

ANTHONY'S LAW OF FORCE:

Don't force it; get a larger hammer.

HORNER'S FIVE-THUMB POSTULATE:

Experience varies directly with equipment ruined.

CAHN'S AXIOM:

When all else fails, read the instructions.

THE PRINCIPLE CONCERNING MULTIFUNCTIONAL DEVICES:

The fewer functions any device is required to perform, the more perfectly it can perform those functions.

COOPER'S LAW:

All machines are amplifiers.

JENKINSON'S LAW:

It won't work.

RESEARCHMANSHIP

GORDON'S FIRST LAW:

If a research project is not worth doing at all, it is not worth doing well.

MURPHY'S LAW OF RESEARCH:

Enough research will tend to support your theory.

MAIER'S LAW:

If the facts do not conform to the theory, they must be disposed of.

Corollaries:

1. The bigger the theory, the better.
2. The experiment may be considered a success if no more than 50% of the observed measurements must be discarded to obtain a correspondence with the theory.

WILLIAMS AND HOLLAND'S LAW:

If enough data is collected, anything may be proven by statistical methods.

EDINGTON'S THEORY:

The number of different hypotheses erected to explain a given biological phenomenon is inversely proportional to the available knowledge.

PEER'S LAW:

The solution to a problem changes the nature of the problem.

HARVARD LAW:

Under the most rigorously controlled conditions of pressure, temperature, volume, humidity, and other variables, the organism will do as it damn well pleases.

FOURTH LAW OF REVISION:

After painstaking and careful analysis of a sample, you are always told that it is the wrong sample and doesn't apply to the problem.

HERSH'S LAW:

Biochemistry expands to fill the space and time available for its completion and publication.

RULE OF ACCURACY:

When working toward the solution of a problem, it always helps if you know the answer.

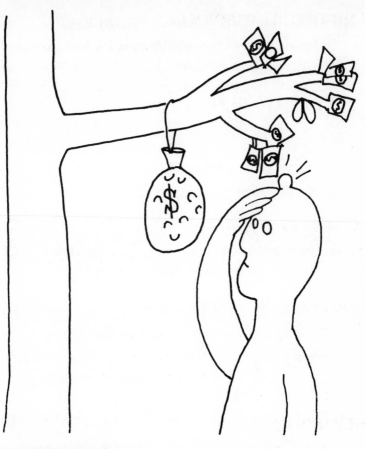

YOUNG'S LAW:

All great discoveries are made by mistake.

Corollary:

The greater the funding, the longer it takes to make the mistake.

HOARE'S LAW OF LARGE PROBLEMS:
Inside every large problem is a small problem struggling to get out.

FETT'S LAW OF THE LAB:
Never replicate a successful experiment.

WYSZOWSKI'S FIRST LAW:
No experiment is reproducible.

FUTILITY FACTOR:
No experiment is ever a complete failure—it can always serve as a negative example.

MR. COOPER'S LAW:
If you do not understand a particular word in a piece of technical writing, ignore it. The piece will make perfect sense without it.

PARKINSON'S LAW FOR MEDICAL RESEARCH:
Successful research attracts the bigger grant which makes further research impossible.

PARKINSON'S SIXTH LAW:
The progress of science varies inversely with the number of journals published.

WHOLE PICTURE PRINCIPLE:

Research scientists are so wrapped up in their own narrow endeavors that they cannot possibly see the whole picture of anything, including their own research.

Corollary:

The Director of Research should know as little as possible about the specific subject of research he is administering.

BROOKE'S LAW:

Whenever a system becomes completely defined, some damn fool discovers something which either abolishes the system or expands it beyond recognition.

CAMPBELL'S LAW:

Nature abhors a vacuous experimenter.

MESKIMEN'S LAW:

There's never time to do it right, but there's always time to do it over.

HIERARCHIOLOGY

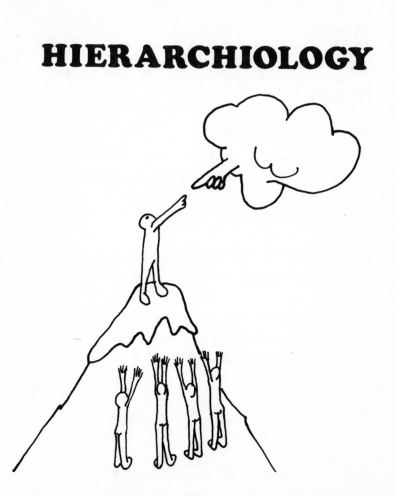

HELLER'S LAW:

The first myth of management is that it exists.

Johnson's Corollary:

Nobody really knows what is going on anywhere within the organization.

THE PETER PRINCIPLE:

In a hierarchy every employee tends to rise to his level of incompetence.

Corollaries:

1. In time, every post tends to be occupied by an employee who is incompetent to carry out its duties.

2. Work is accomplished by those employees who have not yet reached their level of incompetence.

PETER'S INVERSION:

Internal consistency is valued more highly than efficient service.

PETER'S HIDDEN POSTULATE ACCORDING TO GODIN:

Every employee begins at his level of competence.

PETER'S OBSERVATION:

Super-competence is more objectionable than incompetence.

PETER'S LAW OF EVOLUTION:

Competence always contains the seed of incompetence.

PETER'S RULE FOR CREATIVE INCOMPETENCE:

Create the impression that you have already reached your level of incompetence.

PETER'S THEOREM:

Incompetence plus incompetence equals incompetence.

PETER'S LAW OF SUBSTITUTION:

Look after the molehills and the mountains will look after themselves.

PETER'S PROGNOSIS:

Spend sufficient time in confirming the need and the need will disappear.

PETER'S PLACEBO:

An ounce of image is worth a pound of performance.

GODIN'S LAW:

Generalizedness of incompetence is directly proportional to highestness in hierarchy.

FREEMAN'S RULE:

Circumstances can force a generalized incompetent to become competent, at least in a specialized field.

VAIL'S AXIOM:

In any human enterprise, work seeks the lowest hierarchal level.

IMHOFF'S LAW:

The organization of any bureaucracy is very much like a septic tank—the really big chunks always rise to the top.

PARKINSON'S THIRD LAW:

Expansion means complexity and complexity decays.

PARKINSON'S FOURTH LAW:

The number of people in any working group tends to increase regardless of the amount of work to be done.

PARKINSON'S FIFTH LAW:

If there is a way to delay an important decision, the good bureaucracy, public or private, will find it.

PARKINSON'S AXIOMS:

1. An official wants to multiply subordinates, not rivals.
2. Officials make work for each other.

SOCIOLOGY'S IRON LAW OF OLIGARCHY:

In every organized activity, no matter the sphere, a small number will become the oligarchical leaders and the others will follow.

OESER'S LAW:

There is a tendency for the person in the most powerful position in an organization to spend all of his or her time serving on committees and signing letters.

CORNUELLE'S LAW:

Authority tends to assign jobs to those least able to do them.

ZYMURGY'S LAW OF VOLUNTEER LABOR:

People are always available for work in the past tense.

LAW OF COMMUNICATIONS:

The inevitable result of improved and enlarged

communications between different levels in a hierarchy is a vastly increased area of misunderstanding.

DOW'S LAW:

In a hierarchical organization, the higher the level, the greater the confusion.

BUNUEL'S LAW:

Overdoing things is harmful in all cases, even when it comes to efficiency.

SPARK'S TEN RULES FOR THE PROJECT MANAGER:

1. Strive to look tremendously important.
2. Attempt to be seen with important people.
3. Speak with authority; however, only expound on the obvious and proven facts.
4. Don't engage in arguments, but if cornered, ask an irrelevant question and lean back with a satisfied grin while your opponent tries to figure out what's going on — then quickly change the subject.
5. Listen intently while others are arguing the problem. Pounce on a trite statement and bury them with it.
6. If a subordinate asks you a pertinent question,

look at him as if he had lost his senses. When he looks down, paraphrase the question back at him.

7. Obtain a brilliant assignment, but keep out of sight and out of the limelight.

8. Walk at a fast pace when out of the office — this keeps questions from subordinates and superiors at a minimum.

9. Always keep the office door closed. This puts visitors on the defensive and also makes it look as if you are always in an important conference.

10. Give all orders verbally. Never write anything down that might go into a "Pearl Harbor File."

TRUTHS OF MANAGEMENT:

1. Think before you act; it's not your money.
2. All good management is the expression of one great idea.
3. No executive devotes effort to proving himself wrong.
4. If sophisticated calculations are needed to justify an action, don't do it.

JAY'S FIRST LAW OF LEADERSHIP:

Changing things is central to leadership, and changing them before anyone else is creativeness.

WORKER'S DILEMMA:

1. No matter how much you do, you'll never do enough.
2. What you don't do is always more important than what you do do.

MATCH'S MAXIM:

A fool in a high station is like a man on the top of a high mountain; everything appears small to him and he appears small to everybody.

IRON LAW OF DISTRIBUTION:

Them that has, gets.

H. L. MENCKEN'S LAW:

Those who can — do.

Those who cannot — teach.

Martin's Extension:

Those who cannot teach — administrate.

THE ARMY AXIOM:

Any order that can be misunderstood has been misunderstood.

JONES'S LAW:

The man who can smile when things go wrong has thought of someone he can blame it on.

FIRST LAW OF SOCIO-ECONOMICS:

In a hierarchical system, the rate of pay for a given task increases in inverse ratio to the unpleasantness and difficulty of the task.

HARRIS'S LAMENT:

All the good ones are taken.

PUTT'S LAW:

Technology is dominated by two types of people:

Those who understand what they do not manage.

Those who manage what they do not understand.

COMMITTOLOGY

OLD AND KAHN'S LAW:

The efficiency of a committee meeting is inversely proportional to the number of participants and the time spent on deliberations.

SHANAHAN'S LAW:

The length of a meeting rises with the square of the number of people present.

LAW OF TRIVIALITY:

The time spent on any item of the agenda will be in inverse proportion to the sum involved.

FIRST LAW OF COMMITTO-DYNAMICS:

Comitas comitatum, omnia comitas.

SECOND LAW OF COMMITTO-DYNAMICS:

The less you enjoy serving on committees, the more likely you are to be pressed to do so.

HENDRICKSON'S LAW:

If a problem causes many meetings, the meetings eventually become more important than the problem.

LORD FALKLAND'S RULE:

When it is not necessary to make a decision, it is necessary not to make a decision.

FAIRFAX'S LAW:

Any facts which, when included in the argument, give the desired result, are fair facts for the argument.

McNAUGHTON'S RULE:

Any argument worth making within the bureaucracy must be capable of being expressed in a simple declarative sentence that is obviously true once stated.

TRUMAN'S LAW

If you cannot convince them, confuse them.

FIRST LAW OF DEBATE:

Never argue with a fool — people might not know the difference.

LAWS OF PROCRASTINATION:

1. Procrastination shortens the job and places the responsibility for its termination on someone else (the authority who imposed the deadline).

2. It reduces anxiety by reducing the expected quality of the project from the best of all possible efforts to the best that can be expected given the limited time.

3. Status is gained in the eyes of others, and in one's own eyes, because it is assumed that the importance of the work justifies the stress.

4. Avoidance of interruptions including the assignment of other duties can usually be achieved, so that the obviously stressed worker can concentrate on the single effort.

5. Procrastination avoids boredom; one never has the feeling that there is nothing important to do.

6. It may eliminate the job if the need passes before the job can be done.

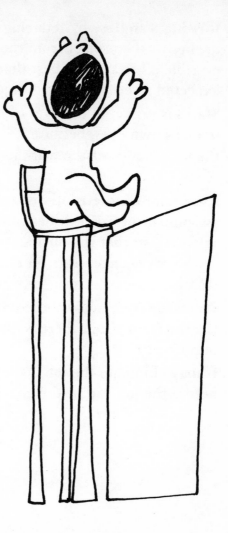

SWIPPLE RULE OF ORDER:
He who shouts loudest has the floor.

RAYBURN'S RULE:

If you want to get along, go along.

BOREN'S LAWS:

1. When in doubt, mumble.
2. When in trouble, delegate.
3. When in charge, ponder.

PARKER'S RULE OF PARLIAMENTARY PROCEDURE:

A motion to adjourn is always in order.

PATTON'S LAW:

A good plan today is better than a perfect plan tomorrow.

ACCOUNTSMANSHIP

FROTHINGHAM'S FALLACY:

Time is money.

CRANE'S LAW:

There ain't no such thing as a free lunch.

PARKINSON'S FIRST LAW:

Work expands to fill the time available for its completion; the thing to be done swells in perceived importance and complexity in a direct ratio with the time to be spent in its completion.

PARKINSON'S SECOND LAW:

Expenditures rise to meet income.

PARKINSON'S LAW OF DELAY:

Delay is the deadliest form of denial.

WIKER'S LAW:

Government expands to absorb revenue and then some.

TUCCILLE'S FIRST LAW OF REALITY:

Industry always moves in to fill an economic vacuum.

WESTHEIMER'S RULE:

To estimate the time it takes to do a task: estimate the time you think it should take, multiply by 2, and change the unit of measure to the next highest unit. Thus we allocate 2 days for a one-hour task.

GRESHAM'S LAW:

Trivial matters are handled promptly; important matters are never solved.

GRAY'S LAW OF PROGRAMMING:

'n+l' trivial tasks are expected to be accomplished in the same time as 'n' tasks.

LOGG'S REBUTTAL TO GRAY'S LAW:

'n+l' trivial tasks take twice as long as 'n' trivial tasks.

NINETY-NINETY RULE OF PROJECT SCHEDULES:

The first ninety percent of the task takes ten percent of the time, and the last ten percent takes the other ninety percent.

WEINBERG'S FIRST LAW:

Progress is made on alternate Fridays.

THE ORDERING PRINCIPLE:

Those supplies necessary for yesterday's

experiment must be ordered no later than tomorrow noon.

CHEOPS'S LAW:

Nothing ever gets built on schedule or within budget.

EXTENDED EPSTEIN-HEISENBERG PRINCIPLE:

In an R & D orbit, only 2 of the existing 3 parameters can be defined simultaneously. The parameters are: task, time, and resources ($).

1. If one knows what the task is, and there is a time limit allowed for the completion of the task, then one cannot guess how much it will cost.

2. If the time and resources are clearly defined, then it is impossible to know what part of the R & D task will be performed.

3. If you are given a clearly defined R & D goal and a definite amount of money which has been calculated to be necessary for the completion of the task, you cannot predict if and when the goal will be reached.

If one is lucky enough and can accurately define all 3 parameters, then what one deals with is not in the realm of R & D.

PARETO'S LAW (THE 20/80 LAW):

20% of the customers account for 80% of the turnover.

20% of the components account for 80% of the cost, etc.

O'BRIEN'S PRINCIPLE (THE $357.73 THEORY):

Auditors always reject any expense account with a bottom line divisible by 5 or 10.

ISSAWI'S OBSERVATION ON THE CONSUMPTION OF PAPER:

Each system has its own way of consuming vast amounts of paper: in socialist societies by filling large forms in quadruplicate, in capitalist societies by putting up huge posters and wrapping every article in four layers of cardboard.

BROWN'S LAW OF BUSINESS SUCCESS:

Our customer's paperwork is profit. Our own paperwork is loss.

JOHN'S COLLATERAL COROLLARY:

In order to get a loan you must first prove you don't need it.

BRIEN'S FIRST LAW:

At some time in the life cycle of virtually every

organization, its ability to succeed in spite of itself runs out.

LAW OF INSTITUTIONS:

The opulence of the front office decor varies inversely with the fundamental solvency of the firm.

PAULG'S LAW:

In America, it's not how much an item costs, it's how much you save.

JUHANI'S LAW:

The compromise will always be more expensive than either of the suggestions it is compromising.

EXPERTSMANSHIP

THE GOLDEN RULE OF ARTS AND SCIENCES:

Whoever has the gold makes the rules.

GUMMIDGE'S LAW:

The amount of expertise varies in inverse proportion to the number of statements understood by the general public.

DUNNE'S LAW:

The territory behind rhetoric is too often mined with equivocation.

MALEK'S LAW:

Any simple idea will be worded in the most complicated way.

ALLISON'S PRECEPT:

The best simple-minded test of expertise in a particular area is the ability to win money in a series of bets on future occurrences in that area.

WEINBERG'S COROLLARY:

An expert is a person who avoids the small

errors while sweeping on to the grand fallacy.

POTTER'S LAW:

The amount of flak received on any subject is inversely proportional to the subject's true value.

ROSS'S LAW:

Never characterize the importance of a statement in advance.

THE RULE OF THE WAY OUT:

Always leave room to add an explanation if it doesn't work out.

CLARKE'S LAW OF REVOLUTIONARY IDEAS:

Every revolutionary idea — in Science, Politics, Art or Whatever — evokes three stages of reaction. They may be summed up by the three phrases:

1. "It is impossible — don't waste my time."
2. "It is possible, but it is not worth doing."
3. "I said it was a good idea all along."

CLARKE'S FIRST LAW:

When a distinguished but elderly scientist states that something is possible, he is almost certainly right. When he states that something is impossible, he is very probably wrong.

CLARKE'S SECOND LAW:

The only way to discover the limits of the possible is to go beyond them into the impossible.

RULE OF THE GREAT:

When somebody you greatly admire and respect appears to be thinking deep thoughts, they probably are thinking about lunch.

CLARKE'S THIRD LAW:

Any sufficiently advanced technology is indistinguishable from magic.

LAW OF SUPERIORITY:

The first example of superior principle is always inferior to the developed example of inferior principle.

BLAAUW'S LAW:

Established technology tends to persist in spite of new technology.

COHEN'S LAW:

What really matters is the name you succeed in imposing on the facts — not the facts themselves.

FITZ-GIBBON'S LAW:

Creativity varies inversely with the number of cooks involved with the broth.

BARTH'S DISTINCTION:

There are two types of people: those who divide people into two types, and those who don't.

RUNAMOK'S LAW:

There are four kinds of people: those who sit quietly and do nothing, those who talk about sitting quietly and doing nothing, those who do things, and those who talk about doing things.

LEVY'S EIGHTH LAW:

No amount of genius can overcome a preoccupation with detail.

LEVY'S NINTH LAW:

Only God can make a random selection.

SEGAL'S LAW:

A man with one watch knows what time it is.
A man with two watches is never sure.

MILLER'S LAW:

You can't tell how deep a puddle is until you step in it.

KAMIN'S SIXTH LAW:

When attempting to predict and forecast macro-economic moves of economic legislation by a politician, never be misled by what he says; instead — watch what he does.

WEILER'S LAW:

Nothing is impossible for the man who doesn't have to do it himself.

LaCOMBE'S RULE OF PERCENTAGES:

The incidence of anything worthwhile is either 15-25 percent or 80-90 percent.

Dudenhoefer's Corollary:

An answer of 50 percent will suffice for the 40-60 range.

WEINBERG'S SECOND LAW:

If builders built buildings the way programmers wrote programs, then the first woodpecker that came along would destroy civilization.

HUMANSHIP

FIRST LAW OF SOCIO-GENETICS:

Celibacy is not hereditary.

BEIFELD'S PRINCIPLE:

The probability of a young man meeting a desirable and receptive young female increases by pyramidal progression when he is already in the company of: (1) a date, (2) his wife, (3) a better looking and richer male friend.

FARBER'S FOURTH LAW:

Necessity is the mother of strange bedfellows.

HARTLEY'S SECOND LAW:

Never sleep with anyone crazier than yourself.

BECKHAP'S LAW:

Beauty times brains equals a constant.

PARDO'S POSTULATES:

1. Anything good in life is either illegal, immoral or fattening.
2. The three faithful things in life are money, a dog and an old woman.
3. Don't care if you're rich or not, as long as

you can live comfortably and have everything you want.

PARKER'S LAW:

Beauty is only skin deep, but ugly goes clean to the bone.

CAPTAIN PENNY'S LAW:

You can fool all of the people some of the time, and some of the people all of the time, but you can't fool MOM.

ISSAWI'S LAW OF THE CONSERVATION OF EVIL:

The total amount of evil in any system remains constant. Hence, any diminution in one direction — for instance, a reduction in poverty or unemployment — is accompanied by an increase in another, e.g., crime or air pollution.

KATZ'S LAW:

Men and nations will act rationally when all other possibilities have been exhausted.

PARKER'S LAW OF POLITICAL STATEMENTS:

The truth of any proposition has nothing to do with its credibility and vice versa.

MR. COLE'S AXIOM:

The sum of the intelligence on the planet is

a constant; the population is growing.

LAW OF THE INDIVIDUAL:

Nobody really cares or understands what anyone else is doing.

STEELE'S PLAGIARISM OF SOMEBODY'S PHILOSOPHY:

Everybody should believe in something — I believe I'll have another drink.

LEVY'S THIRD LAW:

That segment of the community with which one has the greatest sympathy as a liberal inevitably turns out to be one of the most narrow-minded and bigoted segments of the community.

Kelly's Reformation:

Nice guys don't finish nice.

THE KENNEDY CONSTANT:

Don't get mad — get even.

CANADA BILL JONES'S MOTTO:

It's morally wrong to allow suckers to keep their money.

Supplement:

A Smith and Wesson beats four aces.

JONES'S MOTTO:

Friends come and go, but enemies accumulate.

McCLAUGHRY'S CODICIL TO JONES'S MOTTO:

To make an enemy, do someone a favor.

VIQUE'S LAW:

A man without religion is like a fish without a bicycle.

THE FIFTH RULE:

You have taken yourself too seriously.

METALAWS

LES MISERABLES METALAW:

All laws, whether good, bad or indifferent, must be obeyed to the letter.

PERSIG'S POSTULATE:

The number of rational hypotheses that can explain any given phenomenon is infinite.

LILLY'S METALAW:

All laws are simulations of reality.

THE ULTIMATE PRINCIPLE:

By definition, when you are investigating the unknown you do not know what you will find.

COOPER'S METALAW:

A proliferation of new laws creates a proliferation of new loopholes.

COLE'S LAW

COLE'S LAW:

Thinly sliced cabbage.

WALLACE'S OBSERVATION:

Everything is in a state of utter dishevelment.

HARTLEY'S FIRST LAW:

You can lead a horse to water, but if you can get him to float on his back, you've got something.

WEAVER'S LAW:

When several reporters share a cab on an assignment, the reporter in the front seat pays for all.

Doyle's Corollary:

No matter how many reporters share a cab, and no matter who pays, each puts the full fare on his own expense account.

JOHNSON'S SECOND LAW:

If, in the course of several months, only three

worthwhile social events take place, they will all fall on the same evening.

MATSCH'S LAW:

It's better to have a horrible ending than to have horrors without end.

JACQUIN'S POSTULATE ON DEMOCRATIC GOVERNMENT:

No man's life, liberty or property are safe while the legislature is in session.

FOWLER'S NOTE:

The only imperfect thing in nature is the human race.

TERMAN'S LAW OF INNOVATION:

If you want a track team to win the high jump, you find one person who can jump seven feet, not seven people who can jump one foot.

TRISCHMANN'S PARADOX:

A pipe gives a wise man time to think and a fool something to stick in his mouth.

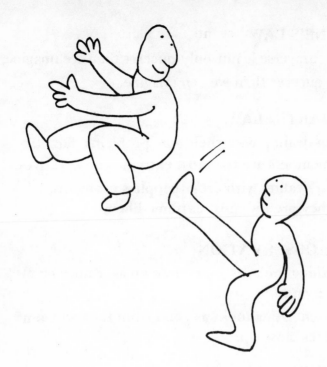

BUCY'S LAW:

Nothing is ever accomplished by a reasonable man.

CHURCHILL'S COMMENTARY ON MAN:

Man will occasionally stumble over the truth, but most of the time he will pick himself up and continue on.

HALDANE'S LAW:

The universe is not only queerer than we imagine, it's queerer than we *can* imagine.

KERR-MARTIN LAW:

1. In dealing with their *own* problems, faculty members are the most extreme conservatives.
2. In dealing with *other* people's problems, they are the most extreme liberals.

LAW OF OBSERVATION:

Nothing looks as good close up as it does from far away.

Or — nothing looks as good from far away as it does close up.

THE AQUINAS AXIOM:

What the gods get away with, the cows don't.

NEWTON'S LITTLE-KNOWN SEVENTH LAW:

A bird in the hand is safer than one overhead.

WHITE'S CHAPPAQUIDICK THEOREM:

The sooner and in more detail you announce the bad news, the better.

Heard a good Law lately? If you have, or if you've come up with a Law of your own, and you would like to see it immortalized in print, why not send it to us? If it coincides with our own experience, there is a good chance we will use it in a future edition of *Murphy's Law*. If the Law you send is from another source, please try to tell us exactly where it came from. Send your Laws to:

Murphy's Law
Price/Stern/Sloan Publishers, Inc.
410 North La Cienega Boulevard
Los Angeles, California 90048